Hello, Family Members,

Learning to read is one of the most important accomplishments of early childhood. **Hello Reader!** books are designed to help children become skilled readers who like to read. Beginning readers learn to read by remembering frequently used words like "the," "is," and "and"; by using phonics skills to decode new words; and by interpreting picture and text clues. These books provide both the stories children enjoy and the structure they need to read fluently and independently. Here are suggestions for helping your child *before*, *during*, and *after* reading:

Before
- Look at the cover and pictures and have your child predict what the story is about.
- Read the story to your child.
- Encourage your child to chime in with familiar words and phrases.
- Echo read with your child by reading a line first and having your child read it after you do.

During
- Have your child think about a word he or she does not recognize right away. Provide hints such as "Let's see if we know the sounds" and "Have we read other words like this one?"
- Encourage your child to use phonics skills to sound out new words.
- Provide the word for your child when more assistance is needed so that he or she does not struggle and the experience of reading with you is a positive one.
- Encourage your child to have fun by reading with a lot of expression . . . like an actor!

After
- Have your child keep lists of interesting and favorite words.
- Encourage your child to read the books over and over again. Have him or her read to brothers, sisters, grandparents, and even teddy bears. Repeated readings develop confidence in young readers.
- Talk about the stories. Ask and answer questions. Share ideas about the funniest and most interesting characters and events in the stories.

I do hope that you and your child enjoy this book.

—Francie Alexander
   Chief Education Officer,
   Scholastic's Learning Ventures

For Barbara
—F.R.

To Lynn and David
—C.S.

With special thanks to Barbara French of Bat
Conservation International, a non-profit organization
dedicated to protecting bats and bat habitats worldwide.

Go to scholastic.com for web site information
on Scholastic authors and illustrators.

ISBN: 0-439-33013-0

Text copyright © 2001 by Fay Robinson.
Illustrations copyright © 2001 by Carol Schwartz.
All rights reserved. Published by Scholastic Inc.
SCHOLASTIC, HELLO READER!, CARTWHEEL BOOKS, and associated logos
are trademarks and/or registered trademarks of Scholastic Inc.

Library of Congress Cataloging-in-Publication Data
Robinson, Fay.
    Flying bats / by Fay Robinson ; illustrated by Carol Schwartz.
        p. cm. — (Hello reader. Science—Level 1)
    ISBN 0-439-33013-0 (pbk.)
    1. Bats—Juvenile literature. [1. Bats.] I. Schwartz, Carol, 1954- ill. II. Title. III. Hello
science reader. Level 1.
    QL737.C5 R63 2001
    599.4—dc21   2001031061

10 9 8 7 6 5 4 3 2 1   01 02 03 04 05

Printed in the U.S.A.   24
First printing, October 2001

Flying Bats!

by Fay Robinson
Illustrated by Carol Schwartz

Hello Reader! Science—Level 1

SCHOLASTIC INC.

New York   Toronto   London   Auckland   Sydney
Mexico City   New Delhi   Hong Kong

It is night.
You and I get ready for bed.
Bats will soon wake up.

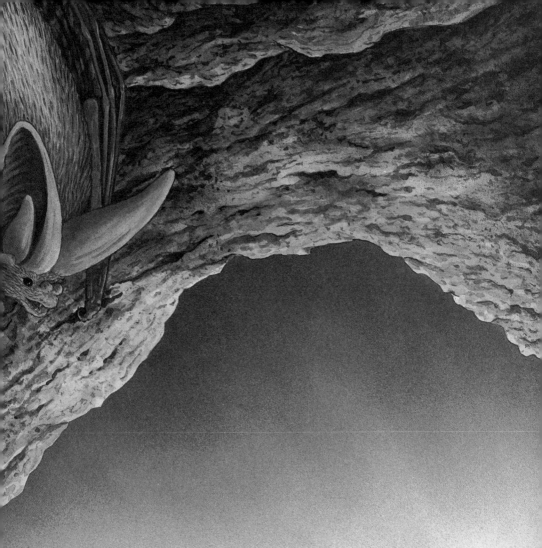

They hang upside down
in caves, in barns,
and in trees.

Now they open their eyes.
They open their wings.

It is night,
and bats fly into the sky.
But bats are not birds.

They are mammals,
like dogs and cats.

They have soft fur.
Baby bats drink
their mother's milk.

13

It is night,
and it is time to eat.
Bats hunt for flying insects.

They catch insects
with their wings

or with their open mouths.

It is night,
and bat pups wait.
They are too young to fly.

Their mothers will come back
to feed them.

It is night,
and bats rule the sky.
They circle.
They swoop.
They dart.
They soar.
Until ...

... it is morning.
Bats are full and sleepy.

They fly back to their caves,
barns, or trees.

They hang upside down.
They fold up their wings.
They close their eyes ...

... just as you and I are waking up.

Cover and pages
4, 8–9, 26–31:
Little Brown Bats

Page 10:
Spotted Bat

Pages 19–21:
Mexican
Free-tailed Bats

Pages 3 and 16–17:
Red Bats

Pages 12–13:
Horeshoe Bats

Pages 22–25:
California
Leaf-nosed Bats

Pages 6–7:
Townsend's
Big-eared Bats

Pages 14–15:
Western Yellow Bats